Martin Bridge
On the Lookout!

Illustrated by
Joseph Kelly

Written by
Jessica Scott
Kerrin

Kids Can Press

For Peter and Elliott. And for Mimi and Papa, who
once surprised us with pink flamingos. With special
thanks to the Nova Scotia Talent Trust — J.S.K.

For Christian and Leslie. You weren't nailed down,
so you're mine! — Pops

Text © 2005 Jessica Scott Kerrin
Illustrations © 2005 Joseph Kelly

This is a work of fiction and any resemblance of characters to persons living or
dead is purely coincidental.

Kids Can Press acknowledges the financial support of the Government of Ontario,
through the Ontario Media Development Corporation's Ontario Book Initiative;
the Ontario Arts Council; the Canada Council for the Arts; and the Government
of Canada, through the BPIDP, for our publishing activity.

Published in Canada by
Kids Can Press Ltd.
29 Birch Avenue
Toronto, ON M4V 1E2

Published in the U.S. by
Kids Can Press Ltd.
2250 Military Road
Tonawanda, NY 14150

www.kidscanpress.com

Edited by Debbie Rogosin
Designed by Julia Naimska
Printed and bound in Canada

The art in this book was drawn with graphite
and charcoal; shading was added digitally.

The text is set in GarthGraphic.

CM 05 0 9 8 7 6 5 4 3 2
CM PA 05 0 9 8 7 6 5 4 3 2 1

Library and Archives Canada Cataloguing in Publication
Kerrin, Jessica Scott
        Martin Bridge on the lookout! / written by Jessica Scott
Kerrin ; illustrated by Joseph Kelly.

ISBN 1-55337-689-7 (bound). ISBN 1-55337-773-7 (pbk.)

I. Kelly, Joseph II. Title.

PS8621.E77M365 2005   jC813'.6   C2004-906567-X

Kids Can Press is a l©rus™ Entertainment company

Contents

Yesterday's Party

Ding dong.

Martin answered the door. There stood Laila Moffatt holding out a big, lumpy present. It was shiny with tape and wore a frilly, lopsided bow.

For once, Laila was wearing a dress. It was bubblegum pink. But something else was different. Martin ignored her wide grin and stared hard.

It was her hair!

Martin knew all about Laila's hair. She

sat right in front of him at school. Her messy orange curls and constant hand-raising blocked his view of the blackboard. But today her hair was combed and held down with dragonfly barrettes.

"Happy birthday!" said Laila.

She turned to wave good-bye as her mom beep-beeped, then drove away.

"You're here for my birthday party?" Martin asked. He couldn't believe it.

"Am I early?"

"No, Laila," said Martin dryly. "You're late. My party was yesterday."

"Yesterday? But the invitation said today. I think." Laila's smile faded.

"No," corrected Martin. "*Yes*terday. It said *yes*terday. I invited the whole class, and they all came *yes*terday."

Laila felt her pockets for the invitation. When she came up empty-handed, she whirled around. But her mom was long gone. Laila slowly turned  back to face Martin. Then she reached for her left foot and pulled it up behind her.

Laila always did that when she was nervous. In that fancy dress of hers, she suddenly reminded Martin of a type of pink bird that stood around on one leg. He tried to remember its name, but his thoughts were interrupted.

"So I missed your party?"

"Yes," said Martin, arms crossed. "You did."

Laila let go of her foot and stood on her toes to look past him, as if expecting to see party guests inside. Martin leaned into the path of her stare until she stood down.

"Well," said Laila in a little voice, "I guess I'll wait on the steps until my mom comes back. She's gone shopping."

She tucked the present under her arm and turned to go.

"No," said Martin glumly, eyeing the gift. "You'd better come in. I guess."

He began to push open the door, but somehow Laila was already inside.

Cripes.

It was hard for Martin to like Laila. She was forever borrowing his pencil crayons at school. Somehow, she managed to sit beside him at lunch every day with her smelly tuna sandwiches. And whenever she got the right answer in class, which was a lot, she'd turn around and smile at him as if they shared a secret. Martin's ears burned just thinking about it.

Frankly, Martin had been relieved when she hadn't shown up for his party.

But now here she was.

All to himself.

"Why, hello, Laila!" said Martin's mom as she came into the front hallway. "Don't you look nice."

"Hello, Mrs. Bridge," replied Laila, and she curtsied. "I thought Martin's party was today." She held up her present as proof.

"Oh, dear," said Martin's mom, her face melting in sympathy. "And look how nicely you wrapped your gift."

Martin looked at the present again. He had never seen anything so overly taped together in his life.

"I picked it out myself," said Laila,
rocking on her heels.

Martin rolled his eyes. "Can I open it?"
he demanded.

Laila clutched the gift tightly to her
chest.

"Where are your manners, Martin?" demanded his mom. She turned to Laila and smiled. "Come with me," she said cheerfully. "Let's go see if we can find some leftover cake." She put her arm around Laila's pointy shoulders and steered her toward the kitchen.

Laila did not look back.

"I'm supposed to go to Alex's house today! Remember?" Martin called. "Stuart will be there, too!"

Alex and Stuart were Martin's best friends. Today they were going to be Park Rangers on the lookout for forest fires. It was their favorite game, after intergalactic missions with their television cartoon hero, Zip Rideout, Space Cadet.

"That can wait," said his mom without slowing her step. "Why don't you set the table for your guest?"

She lingered on the word "guest" and shot him a look that said, "Set the table. Now!"

Martin swallowed hard, lips pressed tight. He took out two plates and glasses, then shut the cupboard doors harder than necessary.

"Fork or spoon?" he demanded as sharply as he could without causing his mom to turn around.

"Spoon, please," answered Laila as sweetly as icing with sprinkles. Martin set a spoon by each plate and plunked himself down at the farthest end of the table. He scraped his chair angrily against the floor and glared at his guest. But try as he might, he could not knock the annoying smile off Laila's face.

Martin's mom brought over what was left of the cake and cut it into two generous pieces.

Martin ate in stony silence.

"Shall I sing 'Happy Birthday'?" Laila finally asked between bites.

"No," said Martin. "We did that *yes*terday."

He licked the last smudge of icing off his spoon and pushed the empty plate away. Laila continued to eat like a princess, one morsel at a time.

"Mom," Martin called impatiently. "Can I see you for a minute?" Without waiting for an answer, he stormed to the living room. His mom followed. "You've got to tell her to go," he demanded. "My birthday was yesterday!"

"I know that. But she's here now. We can't very well send her away," his mom said in a low voice.

"Well, I have plans!" Martin said extra loudly.

"I'm sorry, Martin, but a guest is a guest." She patted his shoulder.

"All done!" Laila called merrily from the kitchen.

Martin sagged in defeat.

"What should we do now?" Laila asked when he trudged back into the kitchen.

"What should we do now?" repeated Martin, his voice a notch higher than usual.

"Yes," said Laila, "until my mom comes to pick me up at four o'clock."

Martin turned to stare at the little hand on the kitchen clock. He counted the hours on his fingers. His Park Ranger fire-fighting plans were going up in smoke! Martin was about to protest, but his mom gave him another look.

"Well," he faltered. "I guess we could ..."

"You could play outside," finished his mom. "It's a beautiful day. Out you go."

She ruffled Laila's hair.

As Laila skipped out the back door, her curls started to spring up. Glowering, Martin followed.

Laila cut across the lawn. Spotting leftover party hats on the picnic table, she put one on and snapped the elastic under her chin.

"Here's one for you," she said, holding out a slightly crushed hat.

"No, thanks," said Martin. "I already wore one. *Yes*terday."

Martin picked up his basketball and began to bounce it on the shimmering hot pavement. Laila did not join in.

"I don't like basketball," she called from the grass, clutching her foot like that pink bird he still couldn't put a name to.

Martin ignored her and shot three
hoops in a row. He missed every time. This
did not improve his mood. He bounced the
ball some more to drown out her voice.
Eventually, he glanced at Laila, who was
now on the swings, head hanging, still
wearing yesterday's party hat.

Martin sighed. He picked up the ball
and reluctantly joined her. They swung

in silence,
except for the
scuffing of
Laila's feet as
she dragged
her polished
shoes back
and forth in
the dirt.

Martin
studied his

swinging shadow. He knew it was nowhere
near four o'clock because the blazing sun
was still high in the sky, beating down on
his neck. It was so bright, it made his eyes
ache. He closed them.

It had been sunny yesterday, too. He remembered how his mom woke him up, covered his eyes and guided him downstairs to the backyard.

"Happy birthday, Martin!" she exclaimed as she removed his blindfold.

Martin stood in his rocket-covered pajamas and looked around. His superhero, Zip Rideout, was everywhere! On the tablecloth. On the plates and napkins. Even on those paper horns that rolled out when they were blown.

As Martin hugged his mom in delight, his dad came into the yard bearing a present. A Zip Rideout Solar System Explorer Set! It had been at the top of his birthday list. That, and a Park Ranger Super-Charged All-Night Flashlight.

He remembered how he played with Zip's set for the rest of that morning, right up until his backyard filled with laughing party guests, music and balloons.

"Say, do you have any balloons left from yesterday?" Laila asked.

Martin opened his eyes and yesterday's party vanished. In its place stood Laila, birdlike on one foot in her pink dress. Only she wasn't about to fly away.

"Why?" he demanded grumpily.

"Go get some and I'll show you."

Martin had no choice. If they didn't find something to do quickly, the afternoon would go on forever. He jumped off the swing and went back inside to the cool of the kitchen.

The telephone rang as Martin searched for the balloons.

"Where are you?" demanded Alex when Martin answered.

"Oh. Hi, Alex," said Martin with a heavy heart. "I can't come over."

"What? Why not? Ranger Stuart's here. We've already spotted our first fire!"

Martin peeked out the kitchen window, hoping this was all a bad dream. Instead, he saw that Laila had unrolled the garden hose and was inspecting the nozzle.

"Something's come up," muttered Martin. "I'll call you later."

"Call me later?" Alex repeated. "When?"

"I don't know. After four o'clock, I guess."

"After four?! But that's the end of the day!"

Martin's heart sank even further.

"Can't help it," he said, and he hung up.

Martin spotted the jumbo bag of leftover balloons next to Laila's present on the counter. The gift was as big and lumpy as ever. Probably something from the all-pink aisle at the toy store to go with that fluffy dress of hers. He started to pick at the wrapping paper, but the tape got in the way.

"Martin!" exclaimed his mom from the doorway.

Martin jumped and bolted for the door. "Just getting balloons," he muttered, grabbing the bag on his way out.

"Be nice!" reminded his mom.

Martin winced.

"Here," said Martin to Laila, not altogether nicely.

Laila opened the bag. On each balloon, Zip's rocket blasted across the sky.

"Perfect," she said.

She fitted a balloon over the nozzle of the hose.

"Now turn on the water," she called to Martin. "Real slow!" Then, "Okay, turn it off!"

Laila pulled the balloon off the hose and expertly tied a knot. She held the balloon up to the sun. The water inside wiggled and sloshed around.

"What do you do with it now?" Martin asked.

"Catch!" Laila teased.

She smiled and tossed it to him. Martin tried to hold on, but the slippery balloon burst in his hands with spectacular force.

"Wow!" he said. "Let me try!"

Martin filled a balloon while Laila worked the tap. But he had trouble tying the knot so Laila had to help. Martin didn't mind. He was too excited about all the possibilities for explosions.

"Let's toss them through the basketball hoop and see what happens," said Martin.

"Okay," said Laila, giggling.

Laila's balloons either hit the rim and blew up or missed altogether. Martin's went right through the hoop before splattering on the hot pavement below.

"EEEEE!" Laila squealed in delight

when their legs got
sprayed.

"Do you think the
balloons will break if
we roll them down
the slide?" he asked.

"Let's try it," she
replied.

The balloons
wobbled as they
skidded down, and
exploded in every
direction when they
hit the ground.

"It's like watching
fireworks," said
Martin, fully
impressed.

"What if we drop them from your tree fort?" Laila asked.

"Great idea!" said Martin.

"How do you get up there?"

"There are two ways," said Martin, shrugging. "You can use the ladder or you can climb the rope." He didn't mention that neither he nor his friends had ever shinnied all the way up by the rope. It was just too hard. And a little bit scary.

Laila chose the rope.

"How am I doing?" she called as she neared the top.

"Great! You're almost there!" whooped Martin, who had grabbed a water balloon and was climbing the ladder.

He reached for Laila's hand and pulled her up through the trapdoor.

"Nice," said Laila as she looked around.

"Thanks," Martin said in awe, still amazed by her rope feat. "My dad helped me build it."

They stood at the window and looked out at the balloon-strewn lawn and water-soaked driveway.

"You first," said Martin.

Laila took the balloon and dropped it from the window. They held their breath.

Down, down, down, down ...

BOOM!

The splatter reached as high as the tree fort.

"Did you see that?!" Martin cheered. "Did you see that?!"

They rushed down the ladder to fill more balloons.

Then one exploded in Laila's hands. Her party dress got soaked, and her wet

curls sprang out in every direction. When that happened, Laila laughed even harder than Martin.

The rest of the afternoon was filled with screams and laughter.

They were filling the last of the balloons when Martin's mom came out with towels and Laila's gift.

"Why don't you open Laila's present, Martin? Her mom will be here soon."

Laila nodded eagerly at Martin.

Martin had forgotten all about the gift. Seeing it now reminded him of how he had treated Laila when she first arrived. Uncomfortable at the thought, he tugged at his wet shirt and looked at his mom.

"Open it," she urged as she plucked a piece of balloon from his hair.

Martin tried to unwrap the present, but it wasn't easy. Laila must have used a whole roll of tape.

"Hurry up, Martin!" said Laila. She sat on her hands and squirmed.

Martin flipped the gift over to attack it from the bottom. More tape.

Finally, just as he was getting the wrapping off, she blurted, "It's a Park Ranger Super-Charged All-Night Flashlight!"

"Wow!" said Martin, freeing the big

flashlight at last. "I really wanted this! I
even wished for one when I blew out my
candles! Thanks, Laila. How did you know?"

"I sit in front of you all day long," said
Laila. "How could I not know?"

Martin said nothing. He certainly did
not know what Laila might like for her
birthday.

Perhaps he should.

There was a beep-beep in the driveway.

"I'm sorry I missed your party," said Laila. She got up to leave.

"Wait!" said Martin. "I almost forgot!"

He ran inside to get the last treat bag. Laila's name was printed on the side, but he had eaten some of the candy when she hadn't shown up yesterday. He hoped she wouldn't notice.

"Here," Martin said as he thrust the bag at Laila.

"For me?" she asked.

"Yes," said Martin, shoving his fists into his pockets.

"Thanks," she whispered, patting down the front of her pink party dress. An awkward silence followed.

Laila reached behind and grabbed her left foot.

Martin smiled. A pink flamingo! That's what Laila reminded him of! Like those one-legged plastic birds that flock to the front yard as a surprise for someone's birthday.

His birthday.

"Sorry you missed my party," he said.
And he meant it. Then he added, "See you
in class tomorrow."

Laila let go of her foot and beamed. She
got into the car and waved good-bye.

Martin waved back.

"Are you coming in?" asked his mom as she started for the house.

"Not yet," said Martin. He lingered in the driveway for a moment, savoring the day. Then he headed to his tree fort and took a long look up.

After a deep breath, and then another, Martin grabbed the rope in both hands and slowly began to climb.

Field Trip

Martin spied his *Tyrannosaurus rex* poster as soon as he woke up. He bounced out of bed, yanked on his clothes and flew down the stairs.

"Today's the day!" he shouted to his mom. His class was going to see the new dinosaur exhibit at the museum. He whooped and gave her a hug.

She smiled as she looked up from the piece of paper she was signing.

"What's that?" he asked.

"Your permission slip," said his mom. "You'll need this to go on the trip."

She set it on the shelf by the front door. "Don't forget it on your way out."

"Not a chance," said Martin.

"I wish I was going to the museum," she teased as she packed her bag for work. "Nothing but meetings for me today."

"I'll tell you all about it when I get home," Martin promised.

She ruffled his hair.

Martin gulped down his bowl of Zip

 Rideout Space Flakes. Then he rushed upstairs to brush his teeth and grab his knapsack.

Hold on! He didn't need his knapsack or even his lunch bag because they were going to eat at the museum cafeteria.

"Bonus!" said Martin to himself as he set down his knapsack and bolted for the door. Without anything to lug, he felt as light as Zip Rideout on a moon walk. Martin jogged easily down the driveway to his bus stop.

"Amazing," muttered Mrs. Phips, his cranky-pants bus driver, as

Martin bounded up the steps. For once, he hadn't kept her waiting.

And yet, as he sat beside his best friend, Stuart, something began to niggle at Martin.

"What's wrong?" asked Stuart.

"I don't know," said Martin. "It feels like I've forgotten something."

"That's because you don't have your knapsack," said Stuart with a shrug. "I feel the same way."

"That must be it," said Martin, nodding.

When they arrived at school, the museum bus stood waiting. Martin's other best friend, Alex, was already on board.

Stuart slid in beside Alex. Martin sat across from them and behind Laila, who was wearing a dinosaur tooth necklace. The engine of the bus began to rumble as their teacher, Mrs. Keenan, climbed on board.

"Wait," she said to the driver.

Instead of sitting down, she counted heads, then riffled through the papers on her clipboard.

"Martin Bridge?" she called out.

"Here," replied Martin.

"Come with me, dear," she said. Martin looked over at Alex and Stuart. Mrs. Keenan only called someone "dear" when they were in big trouble.

Together, they stepped off the bus.

"I don't seem to have your permission slip, Martin," she said.

"Oh," said Martin with relief. "That's because I left it at home. It's on the shelf by the front door where I won't forget it. I'll bring it tomorrow."

He turned to climb back on the bus, but Mrs. Keenan blocked the doorway.

"I'm afraid you can't go without a signed permission slip."

"But it's at home," pleaded Martin, opening his hands to show her they were empty.

Mrs. Keenan looked him over. "Tell you what," she said. "Run inside and ask Mrs. Hurtle to call your mother. If she can talk to your mom directly, I'm sure we can let you come."

Martin didn't wait for Mrs. Keenan to finish her sentence. He bolted through the doors and into the school office.

"Quick!" he yelled. "Call my mom! I need her permission for our field trip."

"All right, all right," said Mrs. Hurtle, the school secretary. "Calm down!"

She fumbled through stacks of paper and pulled out the list of parent phone numbers. Martin tugged at his shirt. It was sticking to his back. As she dialed the number, Martin paced in front of her desk. He could hear the bus rumbling outside.

"Hello. May I please speak to Mrs. Bridge?" asked Mrs. Hurtle. "Yes, I'll hold."

She nodded at Martin and covered the mouthpiece. "They'll see if they can find her," she whispered to him.

Martin rushed to the window and pulled back the blinds. There stood Mrs. Keenan by the bus, looking at her watch. Martin tapped on the window. She looked up and Martin waved. Mrs. Keenan nodded and waved back.

Then she did something totally unexpected. She climbed on board the bus.

Martin watched in horror as the door snapped shut and the bus eased into the driveway.

"No!" he shouted, realizing his mistake. "No! I wasn't waving good-bye! I was waving for you to wait! Wait!!"

The bus kept going. It signaled a left turn as Martin banged on the glass. Then it disappeared down the street, belching exhaust. When Martin finally peeled himself away, he left a forehead print on the window.

"Oh, no. Did the bus leave?" asked Mrs. Hurtle as she hung up the phone.

Martin gave the tiniest of nods while staring at his feet.

"I'm sorry about that, Martin. And your mother's in meetings all morning, so she can't be reached."

Martin slumped in the chair in front of Mrs. Hurtle's desk. His throat felt so tight he could barely swallow.

"The question is, what shall we do with you now?"

Martin shrugged. He wanted to crawl under the desk.

"Wait here a minute," said Mrs. Hurtle. She left the office, her heels clickety-clacking down the hall.

Martin got up and went to the window. Maybe the bus had turned around and come back for him. He pushed the blinds aside and looked out.

No bus.

With that, all hope inside him died. Martin let go of the blinds. They covered him so that only his feet stuck out.

"Ah, there you are," said Mrs. Hurtle when she returned. "I've arranged for you to spend the day with Mr. Horner's class." She said it as if she was announcing they were going to the zoo.

"Mr. Horner? But I had him last year!" Martin wailed from behind the blinds.

"Yes, but that's the best I can do. Now, come along."

Martin followed like a prisoner being led to his jail cell.

"Hello, Mr. Bridge," boomed Mr. Horner when Mrs. Hurtle opened the door. "Welcome back!"

A sea of faces stared at Martin, and there were a few giggles.

"Why don't you sit there, beside Clark?"

Martin's eyes slid across the tops of heads and rested on a familiar face.

Clark.

Martin remembered Clark. Clark was known for eating anything on a dare. Crayons. Eraser shavings. Even paste.

Last year, Clark had been in the same class as Martin. But Clark had missed a lot of school, so he had to repeat the grade. Martin hadn't seen much of him since then.

Clark nodded, and Martin slid into the desk beside him. He could tell Clark was still in the habit of eating odd things. An assortment of gnawed erasers covered his desk. Clark was chewing on one now.

Martin turned away. The girl on his other side gave a tiny wave. Her face was bright pink, and she batted her eyelashes at him. Martin leaned over to read the name on her math sheet.

Zoe Moffatt.

She must be Laila Moffatt's sister. She had big hair, too.

"All right, class," Mr. Horner blared like a foghorn. "Now, where were we?" He proceeded to teach a lesson on adding numbers.

Baby stuff, thought Martin. He scowled.

"Mr. Bridge, perhaps you would tell us the answer to this one," Mr. Horner called, pointing to a problem on the blackboard.

Martin felt a nudge. Zoe handed him a blank piece of paper and a pink pencil with a doll's head stuck on the end. Clark tossed him a soggy eraser with bite marks.

Martin sighed. He took the pencil and used it to push Clark's eraser to the far corner of his desk. Then he scribbled down a calculation and called out his answer.

"Correct," boomed Mr. Horner, giving Martin a thumbs-up.

Martin glanced around. Clark was tearing strips of paper and shoving them in his mouth. On his other side, Zoe was drawing hearts with Martin's initials all over her math sheet.

Martin vowed to stare straight ahead until the recess bell rang. When it did, he trudged outside to the playground.

"Hey, Martin," said Clark as he bounced a ball near Martin's feet. "What's up?"

Martin stood with his hands shoved in

his pockets. Without Alex or Stuart, recess was as dull as the news on television.

"Nothing," he muttered.

"Want to play?" asked Clark.

Bounce. Bounce.

"No, thanks," said Martin.

"Why not?" asked Clark.

Bounce. Bounce.

"I don't feel like it," said Martin.

Clark stood beside Martin and bounced the ball some more. Martin wanted to kick the ball away. Politeness held him back.

"Hey, Clark," someone called from the field. "Show us that ball trick again."

"Got to run!" said Clark.

Martin watched as Clark dazzled the crowd by somehow spinning the ball on his finger. Others began to try. It looked like fun. Maybe if Clark had asked one more time, Martin would have joined them. He sighed and scuffed at the ground.

Martin thought about the permission
slip on the shelf by the front door. He
hadn't known that a piece of paper could
be so important. He had seen his mom sign
a hundred things. Book order forms. Report
cards. Tests he brought home. Nothing
could compare to that permission slip.

His throat tightened. It was getting hard to swallow again.

"Hey, Martin."

Zoe smiled up at him. She held a pink jump rope.

"I was skipping."

"Uh-huh."

"Do you want to watch me skip?"

"Maybe later," said Martin.

"What's the matter?" asked Zoe, her face falling.

"I'm missing my field trip," muttered Martin. "I don't want to be here."

"Oh," said Zoe in a skinny voice. "So you're only with us for today?"

"Of course," snapped Martin. "What did you think?"

"I thought you might be like Clark," said Zoe. She chewed on her lower lip.

"Like Clark? You mean fail a grade?"

"No, I mean like Clark who is a lot of fun," said Zoe, hands on hips. She wasn't batting her eyelashes anymore.

"Clark? Clark who eats erasers?"

"So what? He knows lots of ball tricks. And besides, he makes us things."

"Like what?"

"Things out of tape. He's very good."

"That's ... bizarre!" It was the only word Martin could think of.

"It is not!" said Zoe in a tone like the one his mom used whenever Martin shoved everything under his bed, then told her his room was clean.

"Go back to your skipping," said Martin with exasperation. He waved her away.

"I will!" said Zoe.

She stomped past all the hopscotch games on the playground before spinning around.

"You're nothing like Clark!" she shouted.

The recess bell rang. Martin ducked

into the school and slid behind the safety
of his desk.

"Hey, Clark," called Zoe when she
flounced into the classroom. "May I borrow
an eraser?"

"Sure," said Clark.

He tossed her one. It whizzed past
Martin and plopped on
Zoe's desk.

"Thank you, Clark," said Zoe. There
was a mocking edge in her voice as if she
was going to make a big production.

She proceeded
to vigorously
erase Martin's
initials from
all her hearts.
Martin pulled
his shoulders to
his burning ears.

When Mrs. Baddeck came in with her
music box, there was a mad rush as everyone
jockeyed for the popular instruments.

"Here, Clark. Your favorite," said Zoe,
handing him the tambourine. She managed
to grab the triangle for herself.

Martin hung back, so he got what was
left.

Scratch sticks.

Martin hated scratch sticks. Their

grating sound was bad enough, but even
worse was Zoe ringing the triangle as
loudly as she could right beside his ear.

Mr. Horner returned after music. When everyone settled, he pulled out his chair and sat down. He opened a book and cleared his throat. That was the signal for everyone to lay their heads on their desks and listen.

"Now, where'd we leave off?" boomed Mr. Horner. "Oh, yes. Zip Rideout was traveling back home to Earth when suddenly he had to veer off to dodge a hurtling meteor."

Martin knew the story well. It was the same one Mr. Horner had read to his class last year, and since then it had been made into a movie. After avoiding a collision, Zip Rideout realized that the meteor was now plunging toward Earth's moon.

Mr. Horner read and read. At last he came to a dramatic point. All heads lifted, and everyone leaned forward as Mr. Horner continued.

Zip was trying to send a warning to Earth, but his radio had been damaged by flying debris. The crackling signal got

worse and worse, then suddenly ... silence.

Mr. Horner paused and surveyed the class before clapping the book shut.

"And that's where we'll stop today," he announced.

"Awww!!!" groaned the class.

Martin knew how they felt.

"Don't worry," he called out. "Zip figures out how to trap flying rocks from the meteor's tail into a huge space net, and he swings the net into the path of the meteor. When the meteor hits the rocks, it's thrown off course and misses the moon completely!"

A hush filled the room. Jaws dropped. Eyes widened. The only sound was the scrape of Mr. Horner's chair as he stood.

"Well, thank you for that, Mr. Bridge," he said, his voice as cool as the dark side of

the moon. "I'm sure the suspense would have killed us."

"Sorry," whispered Martin.

The lunch bell rang.

Chairs angrily scraped across the floor, making sounds like a pack of barking dogs.

For the second time that day, Martin wanted to crawl under a desk. He sat until everyone had left the room.

"Martin?"

Martin looked up. Mrs. Hurtle stood in the doorway with Clark.

"Your mom's coming to visit during noon hour. In the meantime, Clark has offered to share his lunch with you."

Martin trudged behind Clark to the lunchroom. They sat near the window.

"Let's see what we have today," said

Clark with gusto. He flipped open his pirate lunch box as if it held a treasure.

"Ham and cheese okay?"

"Sure," muttered Martin. "Thanks."

Martin pried the sandwich apart for inspection. Cheese. Ham. No sign of eraser shavings.

"Martin?" said Clark. "You haven't had a good morning, have you?"

"No," admitted Martin as he took a trial bite. The sandwich wasn't bad. But it wasn't the hamburger he had been looking forward to at the museum cafeteria.

"Well," said Clark. "Maybe the afternoon will be better."

"Fat chance," Martin grumbled. "I'll still be stuck here while my whole class is at the museum."

"Oh. The new dinosaur exhibit." Clark nodded sympathetically. "I heard they even have a *T. rex*."

Martin crossed his arms and frowned.

"Still," said Clark, "we have science after lunch. Mr. Horner always has fun experiments. Remember?"

"Fun?" Martin repeated with an edge to his voice. His face grew red.

Just then Zoe plunked down beside Clark and glared at Martin.

"Well, not as much fun as the museum," agreed Clark, "but —"

"But what?" Martin snapped. "You don't know how it feels to be left behind!"

Cripes. As soon as the words were out, Martin knew he had gone too far.

Everyone stared.

Clark said nothing.

Zoe shook her head and tsked. "Your mom's here," she said flatly.

Martin followed her gaze out the window and saw his mom hurrying across the parking lot. He bolted for the door.

"Oh, Martin," said his mom as she hugged him. "I'm so sorry about what happened."

"Can we go home?" he asked, knowing the answer.

"No, honey. I have to go back to work. But I'll tell you what. This weekend, how about *I* take you to the dinosaur exhibit?"

"Okay," said Martin in a gulpy voice. He wanted to go, but it wouldn't be the same without his friends.

"I hear you're in
Mr. Horner's class today."
Martin shuddered at
the thought of going back.
"Clark's in that class, right?"
Martin shot her a look. "Why?"
"Well, he must be a very nice boy. He got

Mrs. Hurtle to call and ask me to bring you a treat. He said you needed cheering up."

"He did?"

Martin's mom pulled two Zip Rideout Space Bars from her purse.

"Here's one for you. I thought you could give the other one to Clark."

"Thanks," whispered Martin.

After his mom left, Martin sat on the school steps and ate his gooey chocolate

treat. It didn't make him feel one bit better, so he ate the second one, too.

When the bell rang, Martin plodded back

inside. Mr. Horner taught a science lesson on composting, and everyone jostled to pile their lunch leftovers into a bucket of soil. Clark got to stir the concoction while the class squirmed and squealed in delight.

Not Martin. He remained seated and studied the graffiti on his desk.

After a lonely recess during which Clark was nowhere in sight, it was time for geography.

"Pop quiz!" Mr. Horner announced, handing out stacks of tests to those in the front row. "Take one and pass the rest back."

Martin raised his hand. "Do I have to take the test, too?"

"I'm sure you'll do fine, Mr. Bridge," boomed Mr. Horner. "It's material you'll remember from last year."

Martin looked at the questions. They were fill-in-the-blanks. The capital of China is _____. The capital of France is _____. The capital of Mexico is _____.

Martin couldn't remember. Panic made his stomach flip-flop.

He scanned the list. It went on and on.

Martin took a deep breath and picked up his pencil. He filled in some of the blanks, but not many.

Never mind. Mr. Horner always included a bonus question. He would gain marks there. Martin read the question.

Name the oceans of the world.

Pacific. Atlantic. Indian. Arctic. Antarctic.

Good. At least he remembered those.

"Time's up," announced Mr. Horner. "Pass your quiz to your neighbor for marking."

Wanting nothing more to do with Martin, Zoe passed her test the other way. That left Martin with only one option.

Clark.

"Here, Martin," Clark said, handing over his test. Martin took it and reluctantly gave his to Clark.

Mr. Horner read out the answers one by one.

Check. Check. Check.

Clark was getting all the answers right.

Check. Check. Check. Check. Check.

He got the bonus question, too!

"Okay, class. Now add up the marks."

It didn't take long to add because Clark didn't have a single wrong answer.

When he got his test back, Martin's ears burned. Getting the bonus question hadn't been enough. Nine out of twenty was written neatly across the top of Martin's quiz.

Zoe leaned over to look. Then she whispered something to her neighbor. They giggled.

Martin covered his test with his arms. What if everyone found out about his mark? It was probably the lowest in the class! Would that mean he'd have to stay in this grade for the rest of the year? That he wasn't just left behind today, he'd be left behind forever? Cripes!

Martin began to chew on an eraser.

"How did we all do?" Mr. Horner asked jovially.

The class murmured back.

"Zoe," called Mr. Horner. "Any problems?"

"I got sixteen," answered Zoe brightly. She shot Martin a wicked smile.

Mr. Horner followed her gaze and turned to Martin.

"Mr. Bridge," he inquired. "I trust you did well?"

"I ... I ...," stammered Martin. Once again, he wanted to crawl under a desk.

"I marked Martin's test," Clark piped up. "He really knows his oceans."

Martin looked closely at Clark. Was he making fun of him?

But no. Clark merely smiled.

"Well then," boomed Mr. Horner. "Why don't we start packing up? The day's almost over."

Martin folded his test again and again until it was a tight square. Then he shoved it into his pocket along with the two chocolate bar wrappers.

The end-of-school bell rang. After making sure Zoe was nowhere in sight, Martin sidled up to Clark in the coatroom.

"Thanks," he whispered. "You know. About my test." He handed back Clark's eraser.

Clark pocketed it and shrugged.

"But you ...," fumbled Martin, desperate

for Clark to forgive him. "You did really well."

"You mean for someone left behind?" asked Clark quietly.

Martin stared at his feet while Clark looked him over.

Finally, Clark spoke. "Look, Martin. I *do* know how it feels to be left behind, so I made you something at recess."

Martin watched
in awe as Clark
pulled the most
exquisite *T. rex*
from his knapsack.
It was made
entirely of tape.
He handed it
to Martin.

"Thanks," said Martin, his voice full
of surprise.

Clark turned to go.

Martin cupped the dinosaur in his
hands and examined it from all sides.
Clark's gift was as thoughtful as two Zip
Rideout Space Bars. As wonderful as
remembering all the oceans. And as
precious as a forgotten permission slip.

"Wait!" said Martin, looking up.

Clark paused, one hand on the door.

"My mom's taking me to the dinosaur exhibit this weekend," Martin said in a rush, "and it would be great to bring a friend."

Clark turned around with a wide smile, as if knowing where Martin was headed.

Martin pressed on, his voice now full of hope.

"Would you like to come?"

Polly

"Have a seat, boys," ordered Mrs. Hurtle curtly, pushing her half-moon glasses up on her nose.

Martin hesitated. He had never heard the school secretary use that cross tone with him and his friends before. She nodded to the bench outside Principal Moody's door, then returned to the work that cluttered her desk.

Having been dismissed, Martin had no choice but to lead the way to the bench.

Alex and Stuart plunked down beside him.

Once they were settled, Martin glanced
up to make sure Mrs. Hurtle wasn't
looking, then leaned over and whispered,
"Well done!" But he didn't mean it. He just
wanted to remind Alex and Stuart of Polly,
their beloved class parakeet.

"Well done!" she'd say over and over,
just like their teachers did.

Polly was the reason they were in trouble.

Martin replayed the terrible scene in his head. They had come into homeroom before the first morning bell so that Alex could show them his new *Zip Rideout* comic. Polly squawked from her cage when she saw them, which reminded Stuart that

he had crackers in his lunch bag. While Stuart dug the crackers out, Alex came across a mysterious container in his desk.

"What's this?" he asked as he pried off the lid.

A rotten smell filled the room like a low note on a piano long after the key has been played. It was last week's half-eaten tuna sandwich.

"Phew!!" yelled Martin, and he ran to the window. As he pushed it wide open, something flapped by his ear.

He whirled around.

There stood Stuart by the empty birdcage, its door as agape as Stuart's mouth. Stuart was still holding out the crackers.

"Polly! Polly!" Martin called frantically.

"Well done!" was Polly's fading response. "Well done!"

Up, up, up she flew, squawking and flapping, until she was only a speck in the blue sky.

And then there was just blue sky.

Martin slowly backed away from the window, eyes wide in disbelief. He loved Polly.

Cripes, everyone did. And the tragic news had traveled fast. It felt like the whole school had lined the halls to watch as the boys reported to the principal's office.

Martin shook his head at the memory of slinking by all those hostile crossed arms. He squirmed on the hard, unforgiving bench beneath him.

When the principal's door swung open moments later, Martin jumped.

"Come in," Principal Moody growled.

Martin shuffled in first, followed by
Alex, then Stuart. They lined up in front of
Principal Moody's desk. He did not invite
them to sit. Instead, he launched right in.

"I am very disappointed. Polly's been
with our school for as long as I can
remember." He scratched his gray beard.

Martin hung his head. His friends
did, too.

"Who had rotting food in his desk?"

Two fingers pointed at Alex.

"Who let Polly out of her cage?"

Two fingers pointed at Stuart.

"Who opened the window?"

Two fingers pointed at Martin.

"Well then! Since you've all had a hand in this, it's a detention for everyone. Report to the study hall at lunch."

Alex groaned. They played soccer at lunch, and he was their team's star player.

"Make that two detentions each," said the principal, giving Alex a level stare. Then he shuffled through a pile of papers, already moving on to the next problem of the day.

The boys filed past Mrs. Hurtle, heads still down. But in the hallway, Alex shoved Stuart. "Why'd you go and open Polly's cage?"

Stuart shoved back. "Why'd you smell up the class?"

"Stop it! Both of you!" snapped Martin before either of them could mention his part with the open window. He whirled to face them. "We have to find Polly!"

Alex and Stuart shot each other sideways looks, but neither spoke. Martin knew what that meant. They thought finding Polly was hopeless.

The second period bell rang before Martin could say he disagreed, and his friends escaped down the empty hall. Martin hung back, listening sadly to the echoing footsteps until they were gone.

Gone, like Polly.

Martin trudged to class, only to find Alex and Stuart pressed against the blackboard, staring at a sea of angry faces. All conversation had stopped. Nobody moved. Then Laila Moffatt got up and rattled the parakeet's empty cage.

Martin gulped as he and his friends
quietly slid into their desks. There they
squirmed and picked at their fingernails until
Mr. Duncan, the language arts teacher,
walked in carrying a stack of papers.

"Take your places, everyone," he said.

Laila gave Polly's cage one last shake
before returning to her seat.

Mr. Duncan began to walk up and down the aisles, handing back last week's quiz.

"Well done," he said kindly when he came to Martin.

Martin barely glanced at his test. Not even a good mark could cheer him up today. And it was hard to concentrate as Mr. Duncan reviewed spelling rules.

"*I* before *E* except after *C*."

At least Martin knew that one by heart.
So did Polly.

Polly recited spelling
rules with the class all the
time. She would even call
them out during spelling
bees. Sometimes she'd help

too much, and Mr. Duncan would have to
cover her cage so she'd nap.

Martin looked over at Polly's empty cage
and her folded blanket near the window.
His stomach tightened at the quietness of
her corner.

The next thing he knew, the bell rang
and their math teacher walked in.

"Let's keep working on our multiplication
table," said Mrs. Chesterton.

Together, the class called out equations while she pointed to numbers on the blackboard.

"Four times four is sixteen. Four times five is twenty."

"Well done!" cheered Mrs. Chesterton.

Martin remembered how Polly repeated the multiplication table in that squawky voice of hers. She never made mistakes. Smart bird.

But not that smart.

Why hadn't she turned around and come back when she heard Martin calling? Martin could still see her, a little bundle of brightly colored feathers flapping high beyond the schoolyard.

Then recess came. Martin spent the

entire time on the lookout. He wandered
along the school fence, searching the empty
sky. Alex and Stuart followed, still grumbling
about detention.

By the time Martin entered the art
studio for the last class of the morning, his
stomach was a tight ball. And although the
walls were covered with colorful paintings,
all he could see was gray.

"Let's review the color wheel," said Mrs. Crammond as she poured paint into trays. The class gathered around. "Blue and red make ..." She pointed to Alex.

"Purple," he muttered.

"Red and yellow make ..." She pointed to Stuart.

"Orange," he mumbled.

"Yellow and blue make ..." She pointed to Martin.

"Green," said Martin wistfully. Polly was all those colors.

"And that's the color I want you to work with today," said Mrs. Crammond. "Use as many shades of green as you can in your pictures. Begin."

Martin picked up his paint tray and paper and quietly slipped to the far corner of the studio. Then he stared at his blank sheet for a long, long time.

Later, Mrs. Crammond walked about admiring each student's work.

"Well done." She nodded to Alex, who had painted a bright green soccer field with two teams battling it out for the championship.

"Well done." She nodded to Stuart, who had painted an ominous green dinosaur he had seen at the science museum.

She stopped when she got to Martin.

"It's beautiful, Martin," she said in a hushed voice. She stood close to Martin as

they studied his painting. The class gathered
around and solemnly nodded at his tribute.

Martin had painted a picture of Polly
with her exquisite emerald green feathers.

On the way to detention, Alex stopped
Martin in the hall. "I really liked your
painting," he said.

"Me, too," said Stuart. "Maybe you could put it up by Polly's cage. You know, for all of us to remember her by."

Martin smiled at the compliment. And then it came to him.

"I know what we can do!" he exclaimed. "Let's use my painting to make a lost-and-found poster. Then we'll have copies made and put them up all over the neighborhood!"

"Bingo!" said Stuart.

"Maybe we can work on it during detention," suggested Alex. "And I'll call my mom to see if you can both sleep over. That way we can put up the posters tonight." Alex lived only a few blocks from the school.

"If we bring our bikes," added Stuart, "we can cover more streets."

They rushed to study hall. There sat

Mrs. Hurtle at the teacher's desk. It was her turn to be the monitor.

"Can we work on a lost-and-found poster?" Martin asked eagerly. Alex and Stuart pressed in beside him for an answer.

"Great idea!" chirped Mrs. Hurtle in her old, familiar voice. "Let me know if you need any help."

Alex led the way to a corner of the room and pulled three desks together.

"Here," said Martin, rooting through his knapsack for a pen and paper. "You have the neatest printing." He handed the supplies to Stuart.

"Okay," agreed Stuart. "Tell me what to write."

"Lost," dictated Martin. "One parakeet. Answers to the name Polly."

Stuart began to write in big letters.

"L ... O ... S ... T," he spelled. "How's that?"

"Perfect," said Martin. Underneath he glued his picture of Polly.

"How will people tell her apart from other parakeets?" asked Stuart.

"Polly's smart," said Martin confidently. "Write 'Knows spelling rules.'"

"And the multiplication table," added Alex, "and the color wheel."

Stuart wrote as fast as he could.

"Now add the name of our school," said Martin. "And the phone number at the bottom." He was surprised at how quickly the poster was coming together.

Stuart held it up for them to see.

This will work, thought Martin.

Shouts drifted through the window from the soccer game outside. But even Alex ignored the noise. Instead, he and

Stuart nodded intently as Martin reviewed their plan to put up the posters that evening. And knowing that they had a plan made the rest of the school day bearable.

"Hi, guys," Martin called out as his dad helped him unload his bike and sleeping bag at Alex's house after dinner. Stuart was already there.

"Got the posters?" asked Stuart.

"And the duct tape," said Martin, holding up his knapsack. "This stuff sticks to everything!"

The boys jumped on their bikes. They rode around the neighborhood taping Polly posters to everything they could think of. Lampposts. Store windows. Even bus shelters.

They still had some posters left when Stuart looked at his Zip Rideout Rocket Watch.

"It's getting late," he announced.

Martin and Alex nodded and they headed for Alex's.

The next morning, the boys biked to school after a noisy pancake breakfast with all of Alex's brothers. Martin had ignored the clatter and spilt syrup, focusing instead on the mission at hand. When they arrived, he went straight to the school office, Alex and Stuart in tow.

"Any word on Polly?" Martin asked.

Mrs. Hurtle shook her head.

A wave of disappointment hit Martin so hard that he took a step back, bumping into Alex and Stuart. He had been sure their posters would work.

"We still have more posters to put up," reminded Stuart. Martin nodded glumly.

Later, the entire class watched as Mr. Sadler, the school janitor, removed Polly's cage for good. Martin struggled against the

lump in his throat. It felt like Polly was flying out the window all over again.

It was Mr. Duncan's turn as monitor during their second detention. Martin sat in misery, barely noticing when Mrs. Hurtle came into the study hall. She whispered to Mr. Duncan, then came over to where the boys were sitting.

"Principal Moody thinks it might be a good idea if you spent your second detention putting up more posters," she said softly, "so he called your parents for permission. Just be back in time for class."

Martin nodded with new determination while Alex and Stuart grabbed their things.

They continued their tour of the

neighborhood by bike, plastering posters everywhere. When they pedaled by the front doors of Beaverbrook Junior High, Martin pulled over.

"I think we should put up our last poster here," he suggested. "The more kids looking for Polly, the better."

They entered the front doors of the school to get permission, but since it was lunchtime the hallways were quiet. They spotted the sign for the office and were about to enter when Martin clutched Alex's arm.

"Look!" he gasped.

A boy was carrying a birdcage down the hall.

"Holy cow!" exclaimed Alex.

"It's Polly," said Stuart in stunned amazement.

"Stop!" Alex called out.

The boy turned. "Are you talking to me?"

"What have you got there?" demanded Alex, pointing to the cage.

"Our class parakeet," said the boy.

"*Your* class parakeet?" said Stuart. "What's its name?"

"Polly."

"*Our* class parakeet was named Polly," declared Alex. His eyes narrowed and he crossed his arms. "She escaped yesterday."

"Lots of parakeets are named Polly," said the boy matter-of-factly.

"But she looks exactly like our Polly," insisted Alex.

"That's where you're wrong. This Polly is a he, not a she."

Alex and Stuart eyed the bird's feathery body suspiciously.

"Does this parakeet talk?" asked Martin, who had finally found his voice.

"Sure. Polly repeats all kinds of things in class."

"No kidding," said Martin, fuming.

"Well, good luck finding your parakeet." With that the boy disappeared around the corner, birdcage and all.

"Polly," whispered Martin as the parakeet disappeared.

"That's Polly, all right," said Stuart. "Let's report this to Principal Moody." He turned to go.

"Wait," Alex said under his breath, eyes darting left and right.

Stuart rejoined the huddle. "What's up?"

"We're here, aren't we?" whispered Alex.

"So you think we should rescue Polly?" Stuart gulped. "Now?"

"You got it," answered Alex. Suddenly he straightened up.

The boy had returned and was walking right by, empty-handed. "Still here?" he asked.

"Just getting permission for our poster," said Martin, holding it up.

The boy nodded and went out the front doors. Martin turned back to his friends.

It was a crazy plan, but Martin knew they couldn't just abandon Polly. And besides, he had seen Zip Rideout carry out dozens of successful rescue missions.

Martin took a deep breath. "I'm in," he announced.

Together, the boys turned the corner and began to sneak down the hall.

"Think to the brink," whispered Martin, just like Zip Rideout would say when he was right at the edge of danger.

They slipped into the first classroom they came to. One quick look and Martin declared, "No Polly. Let's go."

As they were about to leave, they heard footsteps. The boys scrambled back into the classroom and shut the door with a quiet click. The footsteps grew louder and louder and then stopped right outside the door. Martin held his breath, heart pounding and panic fluttering in his stomach. Someone called out, and a faraway voice answered. The footsteps continued and faded away.

"Maybe this wasn't such a great plan," whispered Alex.

"Yeah," Stuart jumped in. "And who knows? Polly's probably happy learning all kinds of new things in junior high."

But, frightened as he was, Martin was certain it would feel even worse to give up. And he was sure he had never seen Zip Rideout quit. Not once.

"No!" he said with surprising force. "We're here now. And I'm not leaving without Polly."

Alex and Stuart stared at each other and then nodded. Martin slowly opened the door and peered out.

"All clear," he whispered. "Let's split up. That way we can cover more classrooms."

Alex and Stuart took their cue and stepped into rooms on either side of the hall. Martin pressed on and entered the farthest class.

Inside, a teacher's desk stood by the blackboard, piled high with papers. Martin

scanned the rows of desks. There was a
large map of France on the wall, and
everything in the room was labeled with
a French word. The bookshelf. The wall
clock. Even the recycling bin. Then Martin
spied something in the corner.

Something very familiar.

A covered birdcage! Martin carefully lifted a corner of the blanket and peeked underneath. He smiled and ran to the hall.

Alex and Stuart were sneaking toward him.

"I found her!" Martin whispered as loud as he dared. He led the way back to Polly.

Alex reached to lift the blanket, but Martin stopped him.

"Keep the cage covered," said Martin. "If we wake Polly up, she'll start squawking and give us away."

"Good thinking," said Stuart.

The boys ferried the covered cage outside to their waiting bikes.

"Here," said Alex, yanking off a length of duct tape. He fastened Polly's cage to Martin's handlebars.

"Blast off!" shouted Martin.

They jumped on their bikes and started to pedal as fast as they could.

"Stop!" someone called out.

Martin hesitated, feet mid-pedal. But after one glance at Polly's cage, he stood up and pumped even harder.

131

When they arrived back at the school, they hurried to their class and set the birdcage in its familiar corner. Then the end-of-lunch bell rang. The boys rushed to their seats as students began to trickle in.

Laila was the first to notice.

"Polly!" she squealed. "How'd she get back?"

"We rescued her," said Alex as a crowd of students gathered around the cage.

"Let's see," begged Laila, jumping up and down.

Martin was bursting with pride. "Ta-da!!" he cheered as he pulled off the blanket.

"Hello, Polly!" everyone cooed.

"Bonjour!" chirped the strange parakeet. *"Comment t'appelles-tu?"*

Smiles faded instantly. Martin's ears began to burn.

"That's not Polly," declared Laila, backing away from the cage.

"*Très bien! Très bien!*" chirped the parakeet.

It wasn't long before Martin led the way to the now familiar bench outside Principal Moody's door. Alex and Stuart plunked down beside him. They frowned at the parakeet perched in its cage as it mocked them in French from the secretary's desk.

"Ka-boom!" whispered Stuart. It was the word he used whenever something went wrong.

Mrs. Hurtle was on the telephone. "May I please speak to the French teacher? Yes, I'll hold."

Martin sank onto the bench. So did Alex and Stuart. And all three jumped when the principal's door swung open.

"Come in, boys," Principal Moody growled. "And have a seat."

Martin's heart sank. Have a seat, he thought. This was going to be a long one.

"Let's have it, shall we?" the principal demanded as he put the cage on his desk and sat down.

Stuart muttered something, and Alex tried not to laugh.

"Pardon me?" Principal Moody stopped drumming his thick fingers on the desk.

"Maybe Polly flew to France and picked up a few words," blurted Stuart. He tried to smile at his joke, but withered under the principal's glare.

"So you're still insisting this is Polly?"

Martin glanced at Alex and Stuart, who were staring at their feet, saying nothing.

"Well then. Suppose you explain this." The principal reached down behind his desk and pulled up a second birdcage. He placed it beside the first one.

"Polly!" exclaimed Stuart, forgetting himself.

Martin knew Stuart was right.

"Someone found her?" guessed Alex.

"Yes," growled the principal.

"And they saw our poster and called?" Martin joined in.

"This very noon hour," the principal confirmed.

"*I* before *E* except after *C,*" chirped Polly.

"Four times five is twenty," chirped Polly.

"Yellow and blue make green," chirped Polly.

And she kept on chattering until the French parakeet shimmied across his perch to have a better look. Then he began to make soft whistling sounds — the kind Martin's dad made when Martin's mom came down the stairs in a new dress.

"*Ooh la la,*" sang the French parakeet to Polly as she preened her feathers.

There was a tap at the door. Everyone turned as Mrs. Hurtle slipped in with her car keys. She picked up the French Polly.

"Beaverbrook want their parakeet back, *tout de suite*," she said and headed out of the office.

"What do you have to say for yourselves now?" demanded Principal Moody.

"We're sorry," said Martin, and he braced himself for what was to come.

The principal launched into his predictable speech about not leaping to conclusions. About how stealing was wrong, even if they did think it was Polly. And about not fessing up when the evidence was clear.

"So that's a week of detentions for each of you," said Principal Moody.

Alex and Stuart groaned, but all Martin could do was smile.

"Can we take Polly back to class now?" he asked in his best manners voice.

The principal heaved a sigh, and yet Martin thought he spotted the tiniest of smiles.

Martin beamed as he picked up the cage. He remembered the words Zip Rideout spoke on the final leg of every mission.

"Ready and steady," Martin said as Polly looked at him with one eye and then the other. With that he marched out the door, cage held high.

Alex and Stuart followed, shoving each other playfully down the hall.

"Well done," squawked Polly when they entered the class in triumph.

"Well done!" cheered the class. "Well done!"

Martin Bridge Ready for Takeoff!

Ka-Boom!

It was Martin's idea to decorate the model rocket with flames. So why did his friend steal the idea? Now Martin has to come up with something even better in time for Saturday's launch. But will he lose a friend in the process?

Don't miss Martin's first book of adventures, in which his plans for a brilliant rocket, a substitute bus driver and a very old hamster go terribly wrong.

Written by Jessica Scott Kerrin
Illustrated by Joseph Kelly

Hardcover 1-55337-688-9
Paperback 1-55337-772-9

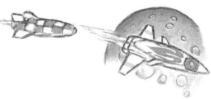